# THE ADVENTURES OF Z:
## Overcoming the dark nights

# THE ADVENTURES OF Z:
## Overcoming the dark nights

Tuwana H. Cummings

Illustrated by Sergio Drumond

XULON PRESS

Xulon Press
2301 Lucien Way #415
Maitland, FL 32751
407.339.4217
www.xulonpress.com

Printed in the United States of America.

Paperback ISBN-13: 978-1-6322-1800-1
Hard Cover ISBN-13: 978-1-6322-1801-8
Ebook ISBN-13: 978-1-6322-1802-5

Be strong and courageous.

Do not be afraid; do not be discouraged,

for the Lord your God will be with you wherever you go.

(Joshua 1:9)

# DEDICATIONS

In memory of Quonziah Caleb Ford, an extraordinary person that left us too soon.

The impact he had on those he left behind will remain forever.

To my amazing husband, Rowhan, and my beautiful children, Londyn and Hudson.

You embody the love of God, and I'm thankful that I get to call you mine.

Finally, to the true author of this book, my Lord and Savior, Jesus Christ.

Thank you for allowing me to partner with you on this amazing project, for your glory.

One Saturday morning before the sun was up, Jacob woke up with his heart racing. The dream he had that night was scarier than the one he'd had the night before. Jacob had been having nightmares for sometime now, and each one seemed to leave him more afraid than the one before. After each dream, Jacob woke up with sweat on his forehead and his pulse pounding. He would jump out of bed and scurry into Mom and Dad's room, where he climbed between them and scooted under the sheets until he felt safe again.

Later that morning, while eating breakfast, Mom asked Jacob, "Did you have another bad dream last night?" Jacob nodded yes. "What was it about?"

Jacob looked down sadly and said, "I don't remember it all, and I really don't want to talk about it."

"Okay," Mom replied. "I understand."

Jacob could remember bits and pieces of his dreams, but he rarely remembered an entire dream, and it gave him chills to even think about them. Even when Jacob was not sleeping, he was afraid to be in dark places because he imagined that someone or something was with him.

Sometimes a lamp would look like a person's shadow, or a tree would look like a monster standing outside of his bedroom window. Jacob couldn't recall when he started being so afraid, but he knew that he didn't like feeling this way.

While Jacob and his mom talked over breakfast, another conversation was taking place in heaven. God was sitting at His own table when He called out to Ziah and asked him to come in for a chat. Ziah, or "Z" as his friends liked to call him, was outside playing football with some of the other angels when he heard God calling him.

**Z** was an energetic angel with a funny sense of humor. Z was just about to score a touchdown when he heard God's voice. "Sorry guys, but I have to leave."

"But you were just about to score one for our team!" said Daylen, one of the angels on Z's team.

"Hold my place," said Z, "we'll pick up where we left off when I get back!"

On his way to see God, Z looked around and thought about how much he loves heaven. He enjoyed playing football with his friends in the large green meadows, next to the beautiful lakes that look like pure crystal. His heart warmed every time he glanced at the buildings made of pure gold and the city wall foundations decorated with precious stones. To look at its beauty is like looking at something out of your dreams, but to Z, heaven was simply, home.

When Z walked into the room, God gave him a peculiar look. Z's wings were covered in dirt because Michael, the team captain of the rival football team, tackled him during the game. God said, "I have a serious problem that will require the right angel to solve it."

Z straightened his wing and brushed the dirt off. "Send me, I know that I can help solve the problem! If You give me a chance, I won't let You down."

"I know you won't; that's why I chose you," said God.

**G**od told Z all about Jacob and explained that he had been having scary dreams and was afraid of the dark. "Fear is real, and I need you to help Jacob to overcome it," said God.

Z stood up straight, put his hand to his brow, and gave a salute. "I know I can do it because You will give me the strength!" God smiled as Z headed for earth to see Jacob.

On Monday morning, the first recess bell rang and Jacob and his friends ran outside to be the first in line for the monkey bars. Earlier that morning, Ms. Byrd introduced a new kid to the class, and he was now waiting in line behind Jacob to take his turn.

Jacob heard a voice say, "Hi, I'm Ziah, but my friends call me, Z. What's your name?"

"I'm Jacob, and everyone calls me... well, Jacob!"

The boys laughed and continued to talk during recess. Later, at lunch, Jacob and Z talked about their favorite sports, the television shows they liked to watch, and which superhero they thought was the strongest.

O n the walk home from school, Z said to Jacob, "What's wrong? You look like you are worried about something."

The closer Jacob got to his home, the more he began to think about the dream he had the night before. By the time Jacob got to his street, his brow was wrinkled and he missed Z's joke about the monkey who could not swing on the monkey bars. "How could you tell?" said Jacob.

"I guess I just know these things," said Z. "Plus, that joke about the monkey not knowing how to swing was really funny, and you didn't even crack a smile."

"**W**ell, I guess I am kind of worried about something. Soon it's going to be dark, and I don't really like the dark."

Z turned to Jacob and said, "I get it. I used to be afraid of the dark, too."

Jacob was surprised to hear this, because sometimes it felt like he was the only kid in the world that was afraid of the dark. Then, Jacob had a thought. "You said that you used to be afraid of the dark. How did you stop? I mean, you know, stop being afraid."

Z smiled brightly. "I asked God to help me!"

Jacob thought about this for a minute. He knew about God and all the stories about Him in the Bible, but he never really thought about asking God to help him to stop being afraid of the dark. He believed that God had more important things to worry about.

The stories in the Bible that Jacob learned during Sunday school, like Daniel in the lion's den and David and Goliath, seemed way more important than his fear of shadows and the creaks he heard in the dark. "Why would God want to help me with something like scary dreams and stuff like that? Doesn't God have more important things to worry about?"

Z chuckled a little and said, "No! Everything is important to God! He wants us to tell Him about all the problems we have, small or big. All we have to do is ask Him."

By now, Jacob and Z were standing in front of Jacob's house. "Well, this is my house. Where do you live?" asked Jacob.

"Not far, just right up the way," replied Z. The boys waved goodbye and went their separate ways.

Later that night before bed, Jacob thought about what Z told him. "He wants us to tell him about all of our problems?" Jacob thought. As Jacob reflected on these words, he sat on the edge of his bed and tried to figure out what he should say to God. Jacob cleared his throat and opened his mouth, but he felt his throat dry up when he tried to speak. Jacob didn't know what to say. He had never prayed by himself before.

Jacob heard the pastor pray at church, and he heard Mom and Dad say grace before dinner. Mom and Dad also said a prayer with Jacob at bedtime, but this was different. Jacob thought to himself, "It's just me and You, God, and I don't know what to say." Jacob decided it was too hard to figure out what to say alone. Besides, he wasn't sure God was listening anyway.

The next day at school, Jacob and Z sat next to each other during lunch. Z noticed that Jacob had been more quiet than usual and seemed pretty distracted. "What's wrong, Jacob?" said Z.

"I'm okay. I just didn't sleep well last night, so I'm still a little tired."

Z realized Jacob was still having trouble sleeping, but why? "Did you pray and ask God for help with your fear of the dark and the bad dreams?" asked Z.

"I tried, but I didn't know what to say," said Jacob. "You see, I've never actually prayed by myself before. I listened to others pray, but, well, I have never talked to God on my own."

**Z**'s face perked up and a big smile appeared on his face. "Talking to God is easier than you think," he told Jacob. "You can talk to Him just like you are talking to me right now. God wants to be your friend!"

"But God is so big, and He's way up there," Jacob said as he pointed his finger toward the sky. "Besides, God's too busy to listen to me anyway," he added, lowering his head.

"Actually, God is everywhere, and He's never too busy to listen to you," Z replied. "In fact, He wants you to talk to Him all the time. I told you, God wants to be your friend!"

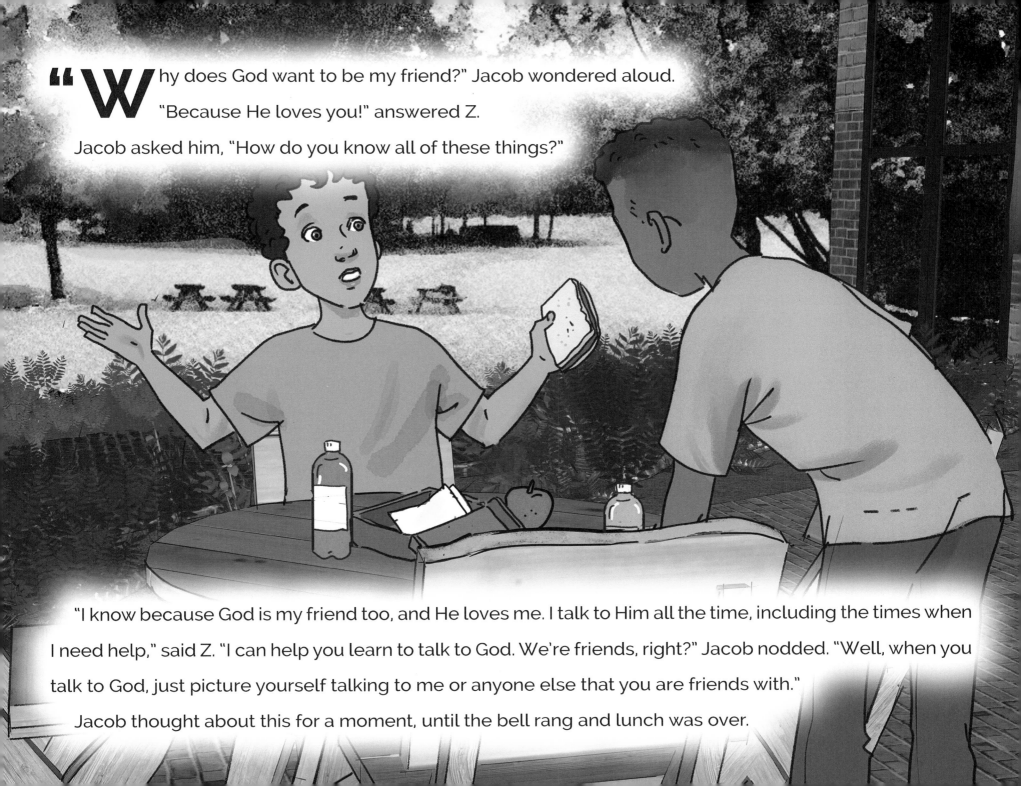

"Why does God want to be my friend?" Jacob wondered aloud.

"Because He loves you!" answered Z.

Jacob asked him, "How do you know all of these things?"

"I know because God is my friend too, and He loves me. I talk to Him all the time, including the times when I need help," said Z. "I can help you learn to talk to God. We're friends, right?" Jacob nodded. "Well, when you talk to God, just picture yourself talking to me or anyone else that you are friends with."

Jacob thought about this for a moment, until the bell rang and lunch was over.

For the rest of the day, Jacob thought about the things that Z had told him. He asked himself, "Does God really want to be my friend? Does He really have time to listen to me talk about my problems, when there are much bigger problems to worry about? I'm just someone who is afraid of the dark." He decided the answer was yes!

Later, as bedtime drew near, Jacob decided that he would try to talk to God again, and this time, he would follow Z's advice. After putting on his pajamas, Jacob kneeled next to his bed. He started to feel a little nervous again, but then he remembered what Z told him about God wanting to be his friend and loving him. Soon, the nervousness went away.

Jacob cleared his throat and said, "Um, hi God. It's me, Jacob. I haven't done this before by myself—talk to You, I mean. But my friend Z told me to give this a try. He said that You want to be my friend and that You want to listen to me and help me with my problems. I want to be your friend, too! I sure could use some help right now because, well, I'm scared. At night when it's dark I feel so alone. I don't like the dark, and I always feel like a monster or something else might be in the dark with me. I don't like to be afraid. I want to be brave and strong, like You! Can You help me with that? Z said that You are everywhere. Are You with me now? I sure hope so." Jacob sealed his prayer with these words: "Thank You for listening. In Jesus's name I pray, amen." Jacob had heard his parents say that last part when they finished their prayers, so he figured he'd better say it, too.

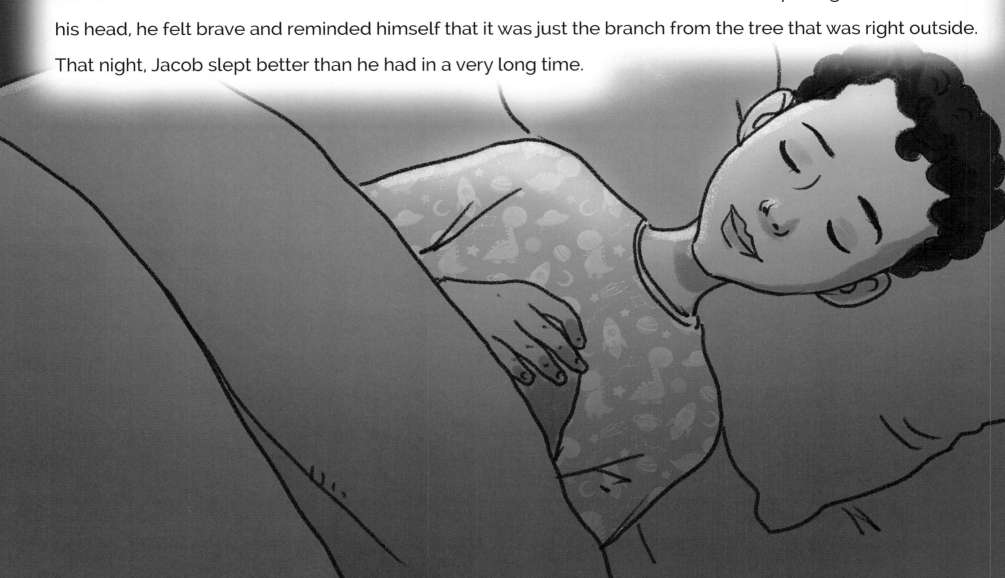

As Jacob climbed into bed, he began to feel something that he never felt before. The feeling he now had was hard to describe, but Jacob sensed that everything was going to be okay. In fact, when he turned off the lamp next to his bed, his heart did not start racing like it had so many times before. And when Jacob laid his head down and saw the shadow from his bedroom window, instead of pulling the covers over his head, he felt brave and reminded himself that it was just the branch from the tree that was right outside. That night, Jacob slept better than he had in a very long time.

The next morning at breakfast, Mom noticed that something was different about Jacob. Mom asked, "How did you sleep?"

Jacob smiled and simply replied, "Great!" Mom saw a joy in Jacob that she had not seen in a while, but from that moment on, it never left.

**A**t school during recess, Jacob ran to the monkey bars where he saw Z waiting. Jacob caught his breath and said, "Guess what Z, I did it, I talked to God just like you told me to!"

Z's eyes grew big and a wide grin appeared across his face. "That's awesome, Jacob!"

Jacob continued, "I was nervous at first, but then I remembered what you told me about God wanting to be my friend and that He loves me. When I remembered that, talking to God became so much easier. After I finished praying, I felt better, and I slept better than I have in a long time."

**Z** looked at Jacob and said, "That's wonderful! I hope you never forget that God is your friend, and He's always willing and ready to listen."

"I won't forget," said Jacob.

He gave Z a big hug, and they spent the rest of recess climbing the monkey bars and laughing at one another's silly jokes.

ater that day, Z went back to heaven. When he walked into the room, God said, "Well done, Z! I knew that I was sending the right angel to help Jacob." Z blushed. "Because of you, Jacob now knows that he can talk to me any time he wants to, and he knows that I'm his friend and that I love him very much." God looked at Z with a big grin and said, "Are you ready for the next assignment?"

"Absolutely! But may I finish my football game first? I was just about to score a touchdown against Michael's team, and I really want to get his wings dirty!"

God laughed and said, "Sure. You've earned it, Z."

# *CONNECTING WITH GOD*

If you don't have a relationship with God, you should know that He desires to have one with you. He's waiting on you to take a step of faith towards Him. Once you do that, God will do the rest! Below is a prayer of salvation based on the scriptures that follow. Once you have accepted Jesus as your Savior, it's important for you to get into a Bible teaching church where you can continue to grow and learn more about the gospel and connect with other believers who will partner with you on your journey.

# PRAYER OF SALVATION

God, You are good, and You love me. I am not perfect, and I confess that sometimes I sin. Sin leads to being separated from You, but because You love me, You sent Your son, Jesus, to take my sins; He gave His life for my sins and gave me a new life in Him.

I believe in You, Jesus, and confess that I need You to save me and take away my sins. I want a relationship with You, which gives me freedom from sin. I give You my life. In Jesus name I pray, Amen.

God loves us (John 3:16)

No one is perfect (Romans 3:10)

Everyone sins (Romans 3:23)

Sin is death but Jesus is life (Romans 6:23)

Christ took our sins (Romans 5:8)

Confess and believe to be saved (Romans 10:9)

People in Christ are free (Romans 8:1)

Lightning Source UK Ltd.
Milton Keynes UK
UKRC010805191220
375207UK00005B/5